# Collins

# Contents

## Unit 10

Core: Swamp Horror ....................... 6

Challenge: Antarctic Survival ................ 24

## Unit 11

Core: The Shore .......................... 42

Challenge: Four Days, Three Nights:
The Rob Hewitt Story ..................... 60

# Swamp Horror

Written by Gareth P Jones

Illustrated by Alan Brown

Ren Wolton loved gaming. His top choice was *Swamp Horror*, a game set on a swampy planet run by killer swans. It was a mystery how the swans had taken over. Other animals roamed the planet too, like wild lynxes that hunted in the mountains. The only humans in the swamp were locked in cages.

Normally, when Ren got home from school, he would run to his bedroom to play. But the game had been down for months, while fans eagerly waited for the new release to drop.

"I'm so excited," Ren told his cousin, Sonny, through his headset.

Sonny was a year younger than Ren, but he was a skilled gamer.

"Maybe in this release we'll get to the bottom of the swamp!" said Sonny.

When the update finally dropped, Ren didn't even say hello to his parents. He just ran to his room, switched on his computer and loaded *Swamp Horror: The New Season*.

"Wow!" said Sonny. "It looks amazing!"

Ren and Sonny chose their avatars.

A message popped up:

Are you ready to begin?

YES NO

Lots had changed in the game. There were new weapons hidden around the map. There were evil monkeys that could kill you with one touch. Some of the young swans had mutated into a squad of cyborgs.

Ren and Sonny's avatars prowled around the swamp, constantly on the watch for enemies.

"This is intense!" said Ren.

"Dinner time!" shouted Ren's mum from the kitchen.

"I'm nearly done!" he replied.

"Watch out. These cyborg swans are going to be a huge threat," said Sonny.

"Whoa!" exclaimed Ren. "It looks like there's a weather system coming in. That lightning looks deadly. We should find some cover."

Ren's fingers twitched. The new update was so good, he couldn't look away. He even had to keep remembering to blink, which was a good sign with a game.

"Hey, gamer-head. Dinner!" called his dad.

"In ... a ... minute!" yelled Ren. "Parents!" he said into his headset. "Am I right?"

"You are not wrong," replied his cousin. "We need to grab a crystal to recharge our health."

"I read on the forum that we'll find out how the swamp was created in this release!" said Ren. "And apparently there's *Next Level Mode*, whatever that means."

"Ren, come down now or I'll switch off the internet!" yelled his dad.

*He's bluffing,* thought Ren.

In the kitchen, Ren's mum and dad were sitting at the table with three plates of pasta in front of them.

"This is ridiculous," said Mr Wolton. "His dinner's getting cold."

"Then he'll just have to eat it cold," replied Mrs Wolton.

"I've had enough of this!" exclaimed Mr Wolton. "These games are too addictive. They shouldn't be allowed."

"We used to play computer games when we were his age," Mrs Wolton pointed out.

"Yes, but not as much," replied Mr Wolton.

"That's because they weren't as good," said Mrs Wolton.

Mr Wolton smiled briefly. "I'm giving him another couple of minutes then I'm unplugging the router."

"Sonny, I'm going to check this ruined tower. Stay in front and watch for trouble," said Ren.

"I've got to go. My mum just called me for dinner," Sonny replied.

"But this could be it!" said Ren. "We could discover how the swamp started and why the swans turned on the humans!"

"Sorry, Ren. I'll see you after dinner."

Sonny's avatar vanished from the game.

"Ren!" yelled his dad. "I won't tell you again."

Ren sighed and hit *Quit Game*.

A message appeared:

He hovered over *YES*, but he couldn't do it.

He clicked *NO*.

Inside the ruin, Ren found a gate. There was a staircase leading down behind it.

Do you want to enter the crypt?

YES NO

"I'm going to switch it off!" yelled his dad.

Ren clicked *YES*.

To enter the crypt, you need to activate Next Level Mode.

YES NO

Ren hesitated. If Dad unplugged the internet router, he'd be kicked out of the game. But he couldn't bring himself to leave.

He clicked *YES*.

When Mr Wolton pulled out the plug for the router, he expected his son to come storming in. But there was no response at all.

"Give him a minute," said Mrs Wolton. "He's probably sulking."

"Ren?" Mr Wolton called. "Ren?" But there was no reply.

When he reached the end of the corridor he found ...

... an empty bedroom! Ren's headset lay on the chair.

On the computer screen, it said:

> Server disconnected. Continue?
>
> YES NO

Mr Wolton selected YES. A new message appeared:

Mr Wolton clicked it away and, to his horror, a figure he recognised popped up on the screen. It wasn't an avatar. It was Ren himself!

There, standing in a dark underground cave, with dread in his eyes, was his son. Ren was trapped inside the game!

# A history of video games

### 1970s: Arcades

When at-home gaming was not yet popular, people gathered to play video games in arcades.

### 1980s: Home consoles

The Nintendo Entertainment System (NES) was released in Japan in 1983.

### 1990s: 3-D gaming

3-D graphics and multiplayer modes marked the rise of 'modern' gaming.

## 2000s: Online gaming

Online gaming services made it easier for gamers to play together or against each other over the internet.

## 2010s: Streaming

New streaming platforms let people show off their gameplay to global fans.

## 2020s +: Gaming goes mainstream

In 2022, the global gaming industry made over $180 billion, making it bigger than the film and music industries combined!

# Antarctic Survival

Written by Liz Miles

**MEN WANTED**

for hazardous adventure.
Low wages, bitter cold,
long months of complete
darkness, constant danger.

E. Shackleton

Shackleton

It's said that Shackleton, an Anglo-Irish sea captain, put this advert in a newspaper. Although the advert has never been found, we know he was looking for a crew to accompany him on an epic trip to Antarctica!

Antarctica is the coldest place on the planet.
A permanent ice sheet blankets the landscape.

Sailors found this continent in the 1800s. Later, people seeking adventure travelled its coast to reach the South Pole, the furthest point south on a compass. Many failed, including perhaps the most famous adventurer: Shackleton.

Shackleton loved the extreme challenges of Antarctica. After failing to reach the South Pole once, he wanted to try again. He dreamed up a perilous plan.

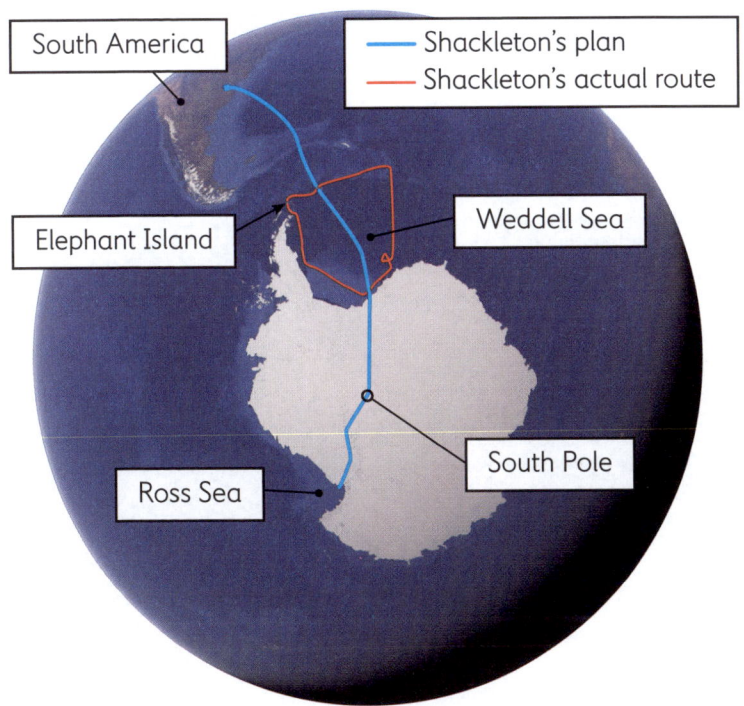

When Shackleton announced the adventure, people gave money to fund it. Five thousand people wanted to be crew members, despite the worryingly long route across such a deadly landscape.

Shackleton picked 27 brave men, including sailors, scientists, doctors and explorers, as well as a cook, a fireman and a photographer.

Sixty-nine sledge dogs and a cat were part of the crew, too!

# Oct 1914

In the summer of 1914, Shackleton travelled from England to South America to begin his voyage. His ship, the *Endurance*, left Argentina in October 1914. It was powered by a steam engine and sails. Shackleton made sure extra thick planks strengthened the bow at the front of the ship. It had to be top quality, as hitting ice sheets could crack it open.

Some sailors wanted the crew to postpone the trip because the sea ice was particularly bad for the season. But nothing would stop Shackleton, so the *Endurance* sailed on.

Shackleton's ship sailed for three months to reach the icy realm of the Weddell Sea.

## Jan 1915

The *Endurance* pushed through the floating ice. Some channels of seawater opened for them, but trouble lay ahead. The pack ice thickened and closed in around the ship until it was halted. Nothing could move it: the *Endurance* and its crew were stuck!

The crew attempted to free the ship by hacking at the ice, but they soon discovered that it wasn't working. Shackleton and his men had to spend the rest of the season waiting for the ice to melt. They had nothing except the supplies on the ship.

Some of the crew tried to shovel a way out.

The battle for survival began. The crew watched for cracks in the spreading ice, hoping for a channel to escape. They slept around a stove to save fuel. Shackleton organised hunting trips to catch animals like seals for extra meat.

The dogs were led off the ship for training. The crew constructed kennels from ice blocks and stuffed sacks with wads of hay to make comfortable dog mattresses.

Shackleton kept his crew active to distract them. The scientists examined rock samples, some of the sailors collected data on wind speeds and the men organised sports games and dog races on the ice.

The sailors read and wrote books.

## Oct 1915

The *Endurance* drifted with the ice sheet for nearly 10 months. The crew survived extreme weather, with blizzards of −30 °C. Their faces froze in seconds. Frostbite was a constant threat. They didn't have phones or a radio, and the closest help was about 2,500 km away.

The tonnes of ice began to squash the ship. Its hull groaned and the decks shuddered. Ice punctured the hull and seawater spilled in.

The *Endurance* was sinking!

The sinking ship symbolised the mighty power of the Antarctic ice.

Shackleton called for the crew to abandon ship, taking the lifeboats and supplies with them. He gave a speech to rally the men, saying, "We'll go home." He wanted to cross the ice on sledges to reach land – but his plan failed.

Getting sledges across the uneven ice was impossible.

Instead, the crew set up camp near the sinking ship. They hoped the floating ice would take them north to safety.

In November 1915, the *Endurance* finally sank.

## Apr 1916

Months later, the crew faced a new threat – the ice sheet began to melt, crumbling under their feet! With no time to waste, the men loaded three lifeboats and began to row with great courage. They had no choice: they had to reach land.

But their attempts seemed to be doomed! Gales turned them back. Then they rowed the wrong way.

At last, the lifeboats reached Elephant Island. Until then, the crew hadn't stood on solid land in 497 days. But many of the men were weak and ill by the time they reached the island. It was barren and no one lived there. They were over 1,300 km away from the nearest inhabited land, so other ships were unlikely to pass by.

An upside-down boat acted as a tent.

Within a week, Shackleton decided to get help. He chose five men and they set off in a lifeboat, which was only about seven metres long. They headed to another island, called South Georgia.

The lifeboat was thrown around like a toy by the rough sea. Waves froze against it. None of the men could sleep in the uncomfortable boat and icy sprays covered them constantly.

After 16 days on the dangerous seas, they reached South Georgia.

Tired and weak, the six men camped for a couple of days, then set off to find people. Three of them stayed behind because they were too ill. The others trekked for about nine days, hiking 64 km across the island. At one point, they realised they were going the wrong way! They climbed mountains and crossed icy pits. They skidded down the last slope on mats made from rope.

## May 1916

Finally, they reached the north coast of South Georgia, where they found people to help. Shackleton quickly organised a ship to pick up the three men left behind. Then he sailed in another borrowed ship to rescue the rest of his crew on Elephant Island. He tried and failed to reach Elephant Island three times – the pack ice kept blocking their way.

## Summer 1916

Two years after leaving England, Shackleton reached Elephant Island and accomplished his rescue. Against all odds, his crew survived!

Despite the deadly challenges, Shackleton achieved his aim: to get his men home safely. The dream to reach the South Pole had been squashed but Shackleton and his crew went down in history for surviving such an epic adventure!

# The *Endurance* is found!

March 2022

Nearly 107 years after Shackleton and his crew abandoned ship, scientists have discovered the shipwreck of the *Endurance*.

Shackleton

The lost ship was found at the bottom of the Weddell Sea, around 3,000 metres below the surface. All things considered, it remains in good shape, with its name still visible on the stern.

The discovery is a great achievement for scientists, who battled extreme weather and shifting sea ice – much like Shackleton and his crew – to find it. They have taken plenty of film footage and photographs, but are not allowed to take any physical elements from the shipwreck. It is a protected monument that must be left in Antarctica.

The survivors of the *Endurance* shipwreck.

# The Shore

Written by Chris Bradford

Illustrated by Jonas Pina

Shawn opened his eyes. He was lying on soft sand, with water lapping at his feet. He turned to see four others sprawled along the shore.

He crawled over. "Hey! You OK?"

A puzzled female face with long hair looked up at him. "Where are we?"

Shawn gazed around. The shore stretched for miles, and a thick jungle edged the beach. The sun was rising above the water.

"No idea," he replied.

"*Please* tell me I'm dreaming," said an older teenager with dark curls.

Beside her, a small boy with glasses blinked at the sunrise. "Were we shipwrecked?"

Shawn frowned. "I don't remember a ship – or any of you."

"I'm Nor," said the older teenager. "And you?"

"Shawn."

"Arjun," added the boy with glasses.

"And I'm Laura. Nice to meet you all ... I think," said Laura, tucking her long hair behind her ears.

"And what about you?" Nor asked.

They turned to a tall figure, walking over to them.

"Hello?" called Nor. "What do you think happened?"

The tall boy just shrugged.

"OK then ... I'll call you Monk," said Nor. "Because you're as silent as one."

Shawn stood up. "Whatever happened, we're in trouble. It's getting hot."

Laura nodded. "We should explore and find help."

They walked along the shoreline, with Monk walking silently behind. A seagull hovered overhead – Shawn could have sworn it had red eyes.

"I just saw a flashing light," said Laura, pointing to a hilltop above the trees. "Maybe it's a lighthouse?"

"Who'd install a lighthouse in the middle of a jungle?" said Nor.

"No idea. But there might be a radio inside," Laura suggested hopefully. "We could call for help."

"Hey, look!" Arjun called out.

They turned to see a wooden crate bobbing in the waves. The seagull landed nearby and watched as they hauled it ashore.

Monk tore the crate open, revealing four water bottles. Nor grabbed one and started gulping.

"Wait, there's only four! We need to split them," ordered Shawn.

"Survival of the quickest," shrugged Nor.

Before they could argue, the crate sank into the sand.

"RUN!" Arjun cried. "It's quicksand!"

They tore across the beach, the sand clawing at their feet.

As they reached the jungle, Laura panted, "Where's Arjun?"

They looked back at the shore. The seagull hovered above, but Arjun had disappeared.

"As I said, survival of the quickest," said Nor, looking troubled.

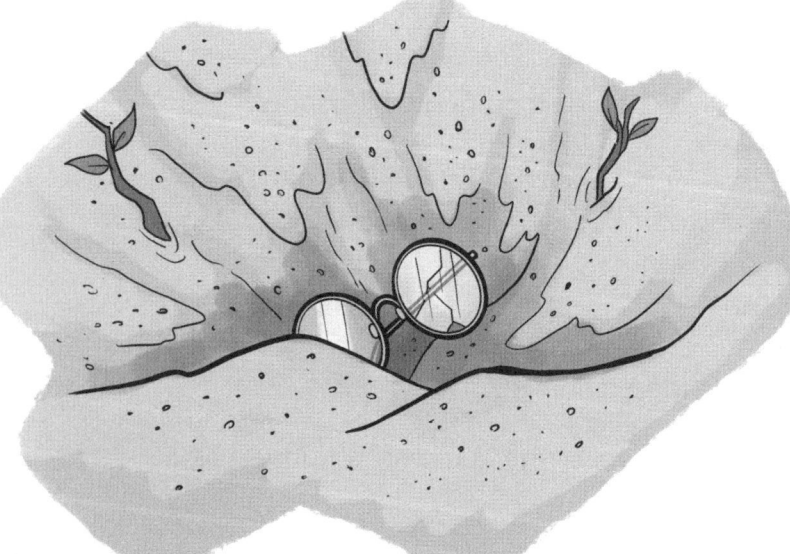

The remaining four trekked through the jungle, battling insects with red eyes and prickly branches that tore their clothes. The heat bore down on them.

The jungle thickened, with vines twisting like snakes.

"We're lost!" Nor moaned. She sat against a tree, while the others looked for a path.

Suddenly, a vine wrapped around Nor's ankle.

"Help!" she called. Her fingers clawed at the ground. But before the others had time to react, she'd gone.

"We need to get out of here!" yelled Shawn.

Monk tore a path through the vines. They reached a clearing as night fell.

Shawn's skin crawled. "This island's like a carnivore ... it wants to eat us all!"

Monk swatted a red-eyed insect that landed on his neck.

*CRUNCH.*

But when he opened his hand, it wasn't an insect they saw.

"It looks like a ... drone?" said Laura. Monk squashed it into the mud.

Haunted by the events of the day, the three took turns to sleep.

When dawn broke, they spotted a temple on a hilltop – with the flashing light on top.

They trekked up to it until they reached a dark tunnel.

"This must be the entrance," said Shawn.

As soon as they were all inside, a gate shut behind them.

"We're trapped!" shouted Laura.

Then the roof began to drop lower … and lower.

Shawn spotted a door ahead. "Hurry!" he called, as he started running.

"We won't make it!" yelled Laura.

"You will!" bellowed a voice behind her. It was Monk, holding up the falling roof!

Shawn and Laura crawled to the door.
It slammed shut, leaving Monk behind.

In front of the remaining two was a rickety bridge, stretched across a pit. On the other side was a silver door marked: EXIT.

"It won't take us both at once," said Laura. "I'll wait for you to cross."

Shawn stepped onto the bridge. It cracked, but it held. He walked across slowly, avoiding any broken planks.

As he reached the end, there was a loud CRACK. Shawn turned his head. The bridge had collapsed ... and Laura was nowhere to be seen!

Suddenly the silver door slid open.

Shawn walked through, into blinding brightness – and found himself in a TV studio, with an applauding audience!

"Well done, Shawn! You survived ... THE SHORE!"

He blinked. "What ... ?"

A woman in a blue suit walked over to him. "Millions of people just watched you get a perfect score!"

The silver door opened again, revealing Laura, Nor, Arjun and Monk.

"Let's make some noise for the other contestants!" the woman said as the audience clapped.

Shawn's mouth fell open. He felt a rush of shock, then relief.

The woman turned to face a camera. "Tune in next week to see who'll join Shawn as the next survivor of THE SHORE!"

# Audience opinions

> Wait ... Shawn managed to win?? That ending threw me. I didn't see it coming!!! I loved the twists – it had me hooked from the start.

**Layla**  5/5

> Poor Monk. Held the roof up like a legend 💪 then CRUSH. Gone. But it was nice to see them all helping each other.

**Max** ⚡ 4/5

> That crate trap? Amazing. Whoever came up with the traps is a genius! Such a clever show.

**Zara**  5/5

> Nor getting vine-snatched was wild. I kinda thought she'd survive. I enjoyed getting to know the contestants but they didn't get equal airtime.

**Tyler**  3/5

> I think it's wrong. Kids dumped on a fake island for entertainment? That's messed up! Did the producers consider their wellbeing??

**Jay**  0/5

> I screamed when Laura fell into the pit! But was it all staged to make Shawn win? Is 'reality' TV ever real?

**Alissa**  2/5

> Man, that bug Monk crushed? A *drone*! We were watching them without their consent.

**Ivana**  1/5

> Finally a reality show with actual drama! Twisted but thrilling! 🔥🔥🔥 Don't like it? Watch something else!

**Malik**  5/5

# Four Days, Three Nights: The Rob Hewitt Story

Written by Susan Frame

Illustrated by Clara Roux

The seas off the coast of Wellington, New Zealand, are famous for strong tides and huge swells. They're made even more dangerous by low water temperatures. But in 2006, one inspiring man called Rob Hewitt survived for more than three days in those perilous waters. This is his story.

## 05/02/2006, Day 1

It's Sunday, and Navy diver Rob Hewitt is on a boat with 11 more divers, out to catch crayfish and kina (sea urchins) off the west coast of Wellington.

But for Rob, a short diving trip with friends develops into in an awful ordeal. He gets stuck in a strong underwater rip current when he dives.

Rob realises he's no longer where his dive began, but he's been pulled much further north.

He watches the captain pick up his fellow divers, leaving him behind.

He considers ditching his diving equipment to try to swim to the boat, but the current is too strong. He can't afford to be without his equipment if he's to stay alive.

A short time later, Rob spots a helicopter overhead. Then he sees boats – lots of them. It's as if they're taunting him as they are looking in the wrong place. He has faith they will find him ... but they don't.

Rob watches them leave.

By the evening, the sea is choppy and the waves swamp Rob, making him feel very small. As the sun sinks in the sky, Rob wonders, *Is this my last sunset?*

Daylight fades.

Rob Hewitt is alone in the sea.

# Night 1

Rob spends the night doing three things: he checks his equipment, then he curls up into a ball on his back with his air cylinder, to retain his energy. Lastly, he talks out loud to all the important people in his life back at home, including his partner, Rangi. He calls out, wanting to let them know he's all right and asking them not to give up on him.

## 06/02/2006, Day 2

After napping restlessly in the night, it's dawn and Rob is wide awake. He hopes that today's the day he'll be saved. It's a public holiday in New Zealand and there's every chance people fishing on boats will see him.

But the swells are almost two metres tall and thick fog rolls from the coast to the sea.

There's not a boat in sight.

Rob now has two battles to deal with: the weather and his exhausted body. The skin on his hands is dying and his face and lips are swelling.

But despite his hardship, his will to live is strong. He pumps blood around his body by performing exercises. He eats raw crayfish and sea urchins from his catch bag. He gets drops of moisture in his mouth from the regulator attached to his air cylinder.

While Rob fights for survival at sea, people gather at his brother Norm's house to co-ordinate the rescue. Norm was a famous player in the All Blacks rugby team, so he uses his contacts to get all the help he can to find Rob.

Police divers are now involved. Their presence gives some people an awful feeling that they're no longer planning a rescue – they're now looking for a body.

## Night 2

Night falls and there's still no sighting of Rob.
It's assumed he has drowned or is in a shark's jaws.
The hunt to find him is called off.

But Rob fights on. He repeats what he did the night before: checking equipment, taking short naps and calling out to his family.

While he dreams of being ashore in his bed, he has no idea his family are planning his funeral.

# 07/02/2006, Day 3

A new day dawns. The sky is blue and the waves have subsided. The weather gives Rob hope, as there's a good chance of swimming to shore. But each time he tries, he blacks out. He feels awful.

Then his thoughts turn to his family. He knows he has to stay alive for them.

The unrelenting sun blisters his face and, under his thick rubber wetsuit, sea lice eat his decaying skin.

Rob slips into a state of nothingness. He's without thoughts and feels almost peaceful. The current begins to carry him again.

Back on land, Norm gets support from the New Zealand Navy, allowing Rob's Navy friends to help find him.

But as they make their way from Auckland to Wellington, a shark makes its way over to Rob …

Dusk approaches. Rob is being tracked by the shark that has now drawn worryingly close to him. His muscles are tired and sore but he knows he must keep still, with his arms tucked in beside his body.

As if by some miracle, the shark leaves.

## Night 3

Rob realises his air cylinder is empty. With no more use for it, he lets it go.

Night draws in and Rob's mind plays appalling tricks on him. He dreams he's ashore and is in a shop getting a drink. He panics when he can't find his wallet and starts thrashing in the water.

Rob regains his senses and realises he is so tired it is causing him to hallucinate. With his energy all but gone, he slips into a dream-like state again. This time, he sees a corridor of light and haunting darkness beyond it. He sees his family and feels their love for him.

"I love you!" he calls out to Rangi and his parents.

As he drifts to sleep, he decides he must do everything to make it back to his loved ones – if he can survive the night.

## 08/02/2006, Day 4

When Rob wakes up, he's astounded to see another dawn. Even more staggering is the fact he can spot car lights back on shore. The current is bringing him back to where he left the boat and entered the water!

By now, Rob is extremely dehydrated. He's absorbed so much saltwater that his whole body is swollen, and his organs are shutting down. He's also hallucinating again, thinking a creature with talons is pulling him out to sea.

He feels suffocated. He rips off his helmet and jacket.

At 3 p.m. the captain of the police launch sees something in the water. He pauses, realising that it's Rob's helmet. Then, in the distance, he spots Rob!

A short while later, Rob thinks he's dreaming again. "What are you doing here?" he says, looking at his friends in shock. Two of his Navy mates have arrived to rescue him!

After being lifted into the rescue boat, Rob takes a gulp of water then tips some over his face. This is the moment he understands fully that – against all odds – he has survived four days and three nights at sea!

# How Rob Hewitt survived

The water temperature off the coast of Wellington is under 17 °C, which is cold enough to kill a human if they stay in it for too long. Rob managed to survive for ten times longer than average for a few reasons.

He was used to cold water diving because of his background as a Navy diver.

He wore a thick rubber wetsuit, which reduced heat loss.

He controlled his breathing and didn't panic or gasp for air.

He rolled up into a ball and didn't move much, which saved energy and body heat.

He had four kina (sea urchins) and a crayfish in his catch bag, which he ate for fuel.

He continued to check his equipment to make sure it worked and to keep his mind focused.

He kept talking to his family and saying their names to reduce worry and keep hope.

**Acknowledgements**

The publishers gratefully acknowledge the permission granted to reproduce the copyright material in this book. Every effort has been made to trace copyright holders and to obtain their permission for the use of copyright material. The publishers will gladly receive any information enabling them to rectify any error or omission at the first opportunity.

p20t Real_life_photo/Shutterstock, p20c robtek/Shutterstock, p20b Pakito/Shutterstock, p21t Ann Kosolapova/Shutterstock, p21c Robert Reiners/Getty Images, p21b robtek/Shutterstock, p24t The Print Collector/Alamy Stock Photo, p24b Nickolya/Shutterstock, p26 Pictorial Press Ltd/Alamy Stock Photo, p27 Pictorial Press Ltd/Alamy Stock Photo, p28 Niday Picture Library/Alamy Stock Photo, p29t CBW/Alamy Stock Photo, p29b Royal Geographical Society/Alamy Stock Photo, p30 CBW/Alamy Stock Photo, p31 Atomic/Alamy Stock Photo, pp32-33 Niebrugge Images/Alamy Stock Photo, p33 (inset) Science History Images/Alamy Stock Photo, p34 GL Archive/Alamy Stock Photo, p35 Science History Images/Alamy Stock Photo, pp36-37 Science History Images/Alamy Stock Photo, p38t History and Art Collection/Alamy Stock Photo, p38b Underwood Archives, Inc/Alamy Stock Photo, p39t ZUMA Press, Inc./Alamy Stock Photo, p39b The History Collection/Alamy Stock Photo, p60 edierdel/Shutterstock, pp74-75 Drew Rawcliffe/Shutterstock.

Published by Collins
An imprint of HarperCollins*Publishers*
The News Building, 1 London Bridge Street, London, SE1 9GF, UK

HarperCollins*Publishers*
Macken House, 39/40 Mayor Street Upper, Dublin 1, D01 C9W8, Ireland

**Browse the complete Collins catalogue at**
collins.co.uk

'Swamp Horror' text © Gareth P Jones 2026
'The Shore' text © Chris Bradford 2026
All other text, illustrations and design © HarperCollins*Publishers* Limited 2026

Wandle Learning Trust name and logo © Wandle Learning Trust

10 9 8 7 6 5 4 3 2 1

A catalogue record for this publication is available from the British Library.

ISBN 978-0-00-879099-8

All rights reserved. No part of this publication may be reproduced, stored in a retrieval system, or transmitted in any form by any means, electronic, mechanical, photocopying, recording or otherwise, without the prior written permission of the Publisher or a licence permitting restricted copying in the United Kingdom issued by the Copyright Licensing Agency Ltd, 5th Floor, Shackleton House, 4 Battle Bridge Lane, London SE1 2HX.

Without limiting the exclusive rights of any author, contributor or the publisher of this publication, any unauthorised use of this publication to train generative artificial intelligence (AI) technologies is expressly prohibited. HarperCollins also exercise their rights under Article 4(3) of the Digital Single Market Directive 2019/790 and expressly reserve this publication from the text and data mining exception.

Authors: Chris Bradford, Susan Frame, Liz Miles and Gareth P Jones
Illustrators: Alan Brown (Advocate Art), Jonas Pina (Astound US) and Clara Roux (Advocate Art)
Publisher: Katie Sergeant
Product manager: Natasha Paul
Education consultant: Charlotte Raby
Project manager: Emily Hooton
Phonics reviewers: Catherine Baker and Abbie Rushton
Proofreader and fact checker: Catherine Dakin
Cover designer: Sarah Finan
Cover images: 2d Alan King/Alamy (front) and GL Archive/Alamy (back)
Internal designer: 2Hoots Publishing Services Ltd
Production controller: Sophie Waeland

Developed in collaboration with Wandle Learning Trust

Printed in the UK by Martins the Printers

MIX
Paper | Supporting responsible forestry
FSC™ C013254

Made with responsibly sourced paper and vegetable ink

Scan to see how we are reducing our environmental impact.

Collins would like to thank Abi Rothe, Nicola Dickens and the schools involved in the Code pilot for contributing to the development of this book.

**Access the planning and resources to teach this book at littlewandlecode.org.uk**